SARAH AND THE DINOSAURS

Aarna Agrawal

*Dedicated to Mom, Dad, younger
brother and grandparents*

PREFACE

2020 is the year when our whole life has changed due to the pandemic. Work from home, online classes and staying at home has become a norm. But this is also the time of opportunities. We get enough time to explore our hobbies, to get creative and to follow our dreams.

From being a passionate reader to becoming an enthusiastic writer, my journey has just begun!

CONTENTS

THE BRACELET

It was a pleasant afternoon. Sarah and her friend Sophia were playing in the park. Sarah was eight years old and was in third grade. Sophia was in her class.

Sarah ran down the grass. Sophia was right behind her. Suddenly, she saw something glittering in the sun. She stopped and took a closer look. It was a bracelet! She wore it on her right hand. Sarah and Sophia played for a few more minutes and then they went home.

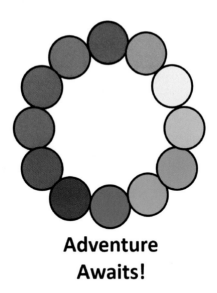

Adventure Awaits!

That night when Sarah went to bed, she forgot to take off her bracelet. It was 9 p.m., but she couldn't fall asleep, because she was thinking about the bracelet she had found in the park. That was when Sarah realized it was glowing!

THE WORDS ON HER WALL

The bracelet shot right out of her hands. Sparkles swirled around it. All of a sudden a letter appeared on her wall! Sarah jumped out of her bed to read it.

The letter said,

Dear Sarah,
You have found this magical bracelet and now you are its keeper. This bracelet will take you to places and adventures from the past and the present. It will also give you magical powers. Just clap twice and say,

Bracelet, bracelet, I found you,
Show me the magic that you can do!

Then you can choose which power you want to activate. To prove you are worthy of this bracelet, it will take you on a mission and you must accomplish it to become its rightful owner. Be careful. Farewell!
Magicland

Sarah wondered about what kind of place Magicland was. Suddenly, the letter disappeared! Sarah's magic bracelet came back into her hands. Sparkles swirled around her. Lightning and thunder crashed. The bracelet was launching Sarah into her first mission!

THE TIME OF
THE DINOS

S arah looked around. She saw a big hill. Wait, it was actually a volcano! Sarah looked in the other direction. She noticed lots of dinosaurs!

All of a sudden a giant T.Rex saw her. It growled and ran toward her.

Sarah ran toward the trees. *I must be in the time of dinosaurs,* she thought. Suddenly, Sarah got an idea!

SPELL TIME!

S arah clapped her hands twice and said,

> *"Bracelet, bracelet, I found you,*
> *Show me the magic that you can do!"*

All of a sudden, a big screen popped up in front of her. It had a list of powers she could choose from.

She chose the one that said *"Animal Talk"*. Then, Sarah could understand what the T.Rex was saying!

"Oh, I am going to get you," growled the T.Rex. "Stay out of my territory."

"Stop!" Sarah yelled.

The T.Rex froze.

"I am here to help you. A volcano is going to erupt and you dinosaurs need to go to a safe place," said Sarah.

"Oh. Thanks for warning me about the volcano," said the T.Rex. "Let me introduce myself. I am Rex."

Sarah said, "Nice to meet you. I am Sarah."

THE PLAN

R ex said, "We need to come up with a plan so that we can avoid lava coming into our homes."

Then, Sarah got an idea! "We can dig a big hole so that all the lava goes in it," she exclaimed.

"Great idea," replied Rex. "We can also go to Dino Hill so that we can be safe. Dino Hill is where we all go for special events and take shelter when the weather is bad," Rex said.

Sarah loudly said, "Let's go!" Then she looked at her bracelet. All at once, a little screen popped up!

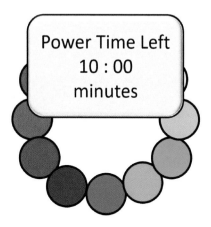

Oh no! I don't have much time left before my power ends! Sarah thought.

She said, "I only have ten more minutes to talk to you, Rex. After that you won't be able to talk to me or understand me."

Rex replied, "Oh. That's okay. I've already got a plan fixed but thanks, you were indeed helpful."

"Ok." Sarah replied.

Then she got on Rex's back and they ran to the other dinosaurs.

Rex got their attention and told them the plan. Everyone got to work. They dug a big hole and made it deep. Sarah helped a little too.

THE VOLCANO ERUPTS

S uddenly, there was a loud rumbling noise.

The volcano is about to erupt! Sarah thought. She was nervous. Then, Sarah looked at the dinosaurs. The hole looked complete and they were starting to go up the Dino Hill.

There is no need to worry. We'll make it to the top right on time, Sarah thought.

She hopped on Rex's back. They climbed the steep Dino Hill. Then there was an even louder rumbling noise. The dinosaurs started walking even faster. As soon as they reached the top of Dino Hill...

THE VOLCANO ERUPTED!!!

FROM LAVA TO ICE

All the dinosaurs took a seat. Sarah sat down in front of everyone. They watched as the lava came down from the volcano.

The lava rushed down into the hole, but there was one problem. The hole wasn't big enough! The lava overflowed so much that it was spreading around the Dino Hill!

Sarah thought about what could happen if the dinosaurs were stuck at Dino Hill. There would be no way to escape. The other dinosaurs in the group also looked very scared. They started chit-chatting about what to do next.

Suddenly, Sarah got an idea!

Maybe, I could get the power to turn things into ice. Then, I would freeze the lava and save the day! Sarah thought. She signaled the dinosaurs to stand back. Sarah clapped her hands twice. The wind swirled around her. She closed her eyes and said,

"Bracelet, bracelet, I found you,
Show me the magic that you can do!"

The screen showed up again and this time Sarah chose the power to turn things into ice. The power got activated and she firmly said, "Turn all this lava into ice!"

The lava immediately froze! The dinosaurs were astonished.

When the lava was all frozen, the dinos cheered. They stomped and danced. Sarah clapped too. Then everyone slid down Dino Hill.

When they were back at the bottom, thunder crashed. It was time for Sarah to go home. She waved goodbye to the dinosaurs, especially Rex. They waved back. Then the bracelet took Sarah back home.

ANOTHER LETTER

In the blink of an eye, Sarah was back in her bedroom and it was 9:15 p.m. As Sarah walked to her bed, she noticed that the bracelet was glowing again! The bracelet shot out of her hands. Sparkles swirled around it. Suddenly, Sarah saw another letter on her wall!

She read it. It said,

Dear Sarah,
You have saved the dinosaurs and passed this mission. You are now the owner of this bracelet. Every evening at bedtime, the bracelet will take you on a mission. After completing five missions, it will take you on an adventure. Remember, don't tell anyone about this or the bracelet will disappear.
Magicland

Sarah sighed. She was really tired but she was also thinking about the letter on her wall. Sarah wondered about Magicland. Then she fell asleep.

Hope You Enjoyed This Book!

Stay tuned for the next adventure of Sarah and the magic bracelet!

♥ tauna

Made in the USA
Columbia, SC
06 September 2022

66690920R00015